D1234718

NINJA
WAR FOR THE DOMINIONS

WAR FOR THE DOMINIONS

VOLUME 2

TYLER "NINJA" BLEVINS
AND **JUSTIN JORDAN**

ART BY **MIKE ANDERSON**
AND **FELIPE MAGAÑA**

COLORS BY BRAD SIMPSON

LETTERING BY CARLOS M. MANGUAL

TEN SPEED PRESS
California | New York

"THE KETTERUNG IS EMPTY.

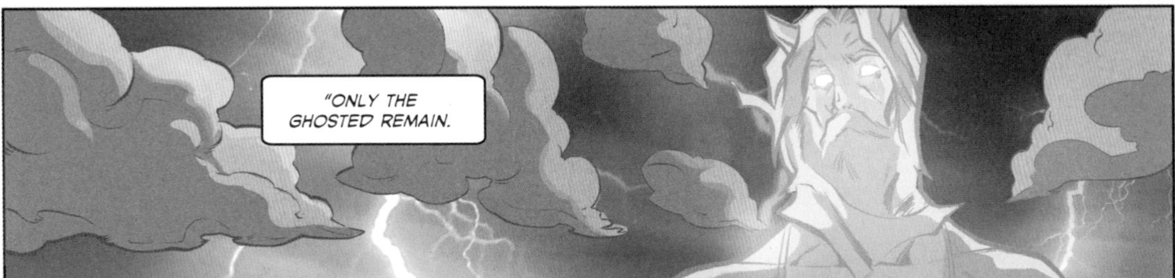
"ONLY THE GHOSTED REMAIN.

"AND WITHOUT THE GAME, THE DOMINIONS HAVE TURNED ON EACH OTHER.

"BROTHER AGAINST BROTHER.

"THERE IS CHAOS."

BUT DO NOT WORRY. THERE IS HOPE.
THE DOMINION PEACEMAKERS HAVE KEPT US SAFE.
"STRIGUS THULE HAS KEPT US SAFE."
AND TOGETHER WE ARE STRONG.

"WE KNOW RIGHT NOW THAT THE ACTIONS OF THESE TERRORISTS AND CRIMINALS HAVE YOU AFRAID.

"THEY HAVE DISRUPTED OUR PEACE AND DESTROYED THE SOCIETY STRIGUS THULE HAS WORKED SO HARD TO BUILD.

"BUT EVEN AS WE SPEAK, SOLDIERS ARE RETAKING THE STREETS.

"LED BY THE GREAT BEAST, WE WILL BRING ORDER TO THE THOUSAND DOMINIONS ONCE MORE."

"THE PEACE OF STRIGUS THULE WILL BE RESTORED.

"THERE MAY BE SOME DISRUPTION TO ORDINARY ACTIVITIES.

"BUT DO NOT WORRY. ONLY REBELS HAVE ANYTHING TO FEAR."

COME ON.

YOU CAN'T.

THEY...
WE CAN'T FIGHT THEM.
YOU KNOW...

...I WAS GOING TO GIVE YOU A CHANCE TO SURRENDER.

BUT I THINK I'M GOING TO JUST SKIP STRAIGHT TO THE BUTT KICKING.
NINJA.
OKAY, FOR ONCE, THAT'S A PLAN I CAN GET BEHIND.
YOU SHOULD GET BEHIND MY SHIELD, DOZER. THESE GUYS HAVE MORE THAN JUST SWORDS.
BUT DO THEY HAVE AN AWESOME HAMMER, LIZARD?

I DO NOT KNOW IF THE MANIFEST SWORDS ARE GOING TO HOLD UP. THEY ARE NOT DESIGNED FOR THIS.

YES, WELL, WE MAKE DO WITH WHAT WE HAVE.
WHAT THEY HAVE IS AN ARMY.
DO NOT WORRY...

"...WE HAVE
NINJA."

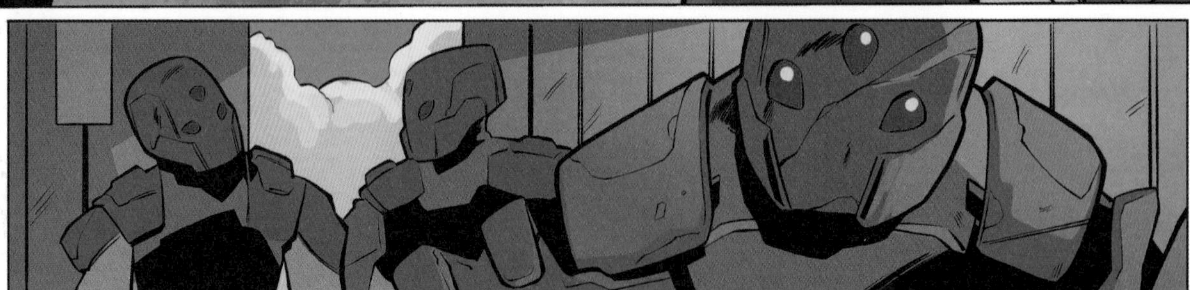

I DO NOT THINK THAT WILL BE ENOUGH.
THEN HELP THEM INSTEAD OF DISTRACTING ME.

WHUMP
ALL RIGHT THEN, WHO'S...
...NEXT?
YOU.

I AM THINKING HE IS NOT.

I HAVE TO ADMIT...
...YOU ARE TOTALLY BETTER THAN A SWORD, HB.
NO, I AM NOT GIVING HIM UP. I KNOW YOU DON'T LIKE HIM. HE DOESN'T LIKE YOU EITHER.
SO, THAT WAS KIND OF AWESOME.
WE CANNOT ALL BE NINJA, BUT I TRY.
I COULD HAVE HANDLED IT.

THIS ISN'T SAFE.
I'M NOT SURE OVERTHROWING EVIL INTERDIMENSIONAL DICTATORS IS MEANT TO BE SAFE.
I WON'T LET ANYTHING HAPPEN TO YOU. I CAN'T. NOT AFTER WHAT I DID.

LIZARD... LIZA, I'M NOT YOUR RESPONSIBILITY. YOU DON'T OWE ME ANYTHING.
I OWE YOU EVERYTHING. IF I'D STAYED WITH KELLER...
BUT YOU DIDN'T. SO CAN WE START FOCUSING ON WINNING THIS FIGHT?
THERE ARE HUNDREDS OF THESE GUYS.
NAH. PROBABLY THOUSANDS.
NOT ACTUALLY HELPING. WE CAN'T WIN THIS, NOT ALONE.

WELL THEN, I GUESS IT'S GOOD WE'RE NOT ALONE.

WE'RE TOGETHER.
MY NAME IS NINJA, AND I'M NOT PLAYING STRIGUS THULE'S GAME.
I'LL FIGHT HIM. HIS SOLDIERS, HIS GREAT BEASTS, ALL OF IT.
BUT I WON'T WIN. I CAN'T WIN THIS.

NOT ALONE.
BUT THESE AREN'T MONSTERS. THEY AREN'T INVINCIBLE.
THEY'RE JUST PEOPLE. JUST LIKE YOU.
JUST LIKE ME. I CAN'T BEAT THEM ALONE.
BUT WE CAN.

"YOU CAN."
SO, THAT SEEMED TO WORK.
WE'RE NOT DONE YET.
COME ON!

RUN.

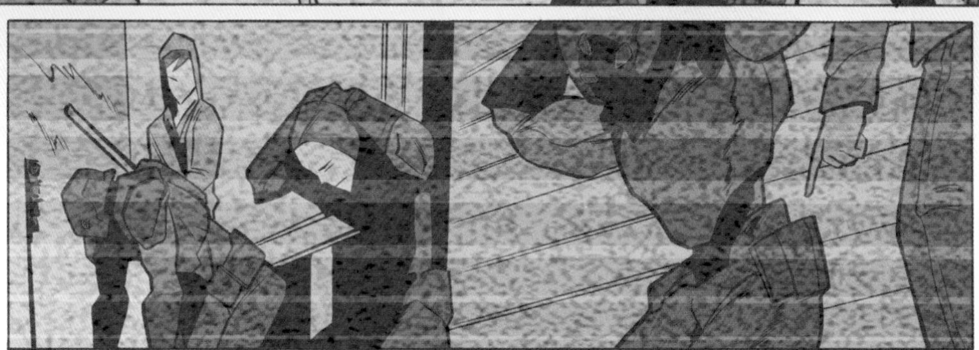

WHY?

WHY AREN'T YOU THERE?
BECAUSE IT WOULD BE POINTLESS.
WINNING IS POINTLESS?
YOU ARE PLAYING THE WRONG GAME, NINJA ISN'T TRYING TO WIN BATTLES.

THE FEED WOULD SEEM TO INDICATE THAT YOU ARE WRONG ABOUT THAT.
THE BATTLE IS SECONDARY. HE IS FIGHTING FOR HEARTS AND MINDS.
AND HE IS WINNING.
I DO NOT KNOW WHY STRIGUS ALLOWS THIS FARCE TO CONTINUE. BUT I DO KNOW WHY YOU DO NOT FIGHT.
BECAUSE YOU ARE AFRAID. YOU HAD EVERY ADVANTAGE ON THE KETTERUNG, AND NINJA STILL PREVAILED.

HE GHOSTED YOU, AND ONLY BY MY BROTHER'S GRACE DO YOU STAND HERE NOW. YOU--
YOU SHOULD CONSIDER YOUR NEXT WORDS CAREFULLY.

AND... YOU...SHOULD CONSIDER YOUR ACTIONS.

STRIGUS THULE IS ALWAYS WATCHING.
GASP
I DO NOT KNEEL.
DO YOU DIE? YOU WERE GOING TO LAY HANDS ON--
I WAS. BECAUSE I NEED TO GET THE ATTENTION OF THE ZERO BEAST. OF THE GOD OF GAMES. OF YOU, STRIGUS THULE.
YOU DO NOT SPEAK TO HIM.
SOMEONE SHOULD.
YOU COULD KILL NINJA. BUT YOU WOULD ONLY KILL THE MAN. WHAT HE'S STARTED WOULD ONLY GROW STRONGER.
I CAN DO WHAT NEEDS TO BE DONE. GIVE ME CONTROL OF THE FEED. I WILL DESTROY THE MAN, BUT FIRST?
I WILL DESTROY THE LEGEND.

YES.

YOU WOULD NOT. YOU CANNOT.
GO.
THIS IS UNFAIR. I CREATED THE FEED. I HAVE PUSHED THE LEGEND OF STRIGUS THULE ACROSS THE THOUSAND DOMINIONS. YOU CAN'T JUST GIVE IT AWAY.
WE BUILT THIS TOGETHER.
WE?
THERE IS NO "WE."

THIS IS WHAT YOU WANTED, ISN'T IT?

IT MUST BE. YOU WOULD DEFY STRIGUS THULE? YOU WOULD CHOOSE CHAOS OVER ORDER? WAR OVER PEACE?
THEN YOU MUST HAVE WANTED THIS. MARTYRS TO A HOPELESS CAUSE.

"I AM HAPPY TO OBLIGE."

ALL THE DOMINIONS ARE WATCHING.

WHERE TO START?

SO MANY CHOICES. WOULD ANY OF YOU LIKE TO VOLUNTEER?
NO?
CSDESIS.

JUST GET THIS OVER WITH. I'M TOO OLD TO SPEND ALL DAY ON MY KNEES.

OH, I LIKE YOU. AND I SAID BEFORE...

...I AM HAPPY TO OBLIGE.

DUDE...

...DO YOU
EVER STOP
TALKING?
BECAUSE
I AM SICK OF
IT ALREADY.
"AND I'M
PRETTY SURE THEY
ARE TOO."

NINJA. FINALLY.
KEEP THE CIVILIANS SAFE AND KEEP THOSE SOLDIERS OFF OF ME. I'LL TAKE THIS CSDESIS GUY.
ON IT.
WELL, ARE YOU GOING TO FIGHT OR...

WHAT?!
DID YOU FORGET THE EPIC WEAPONS ARE ALIVE?
BECAUSE I DIDN'T.
AHHHH!
NINJA!
DON'T YOU TOUCH HIM.

AH, TEAMWORK.
NO!
YES, THANK YOU FOR THE ASSIST.

COME ON.

I AM. AND YOU ARE GOING.

NOT YET.

STAY DOWN.

I CAN'T KEEP THIS UP FOREVER. ALMOST FOREVER, SURE.

YOU DIDN'T HAVE TO DO THAT.
THAT'S A FUNNY WAY TO SAY THANK YOU. AND YES, I CLEARLY DID.

YOU ARE GETTING INCREDIBLY TEDIOUS.

YES. I KNOW YOU'RE DOING YOUR BEST, HB. YOU TAKE CARE OF THIS.

"I'LL TAKE CARE OF HIM."
IF YOU WANT TO DIE THAT BADLY, WOMAN, I CAN OBLIGE.

NO, YOU WON'T.
YOU DESERVE THIS. WORSE THAN THIS. WHAT YOU DID TO THOSE PEOPLE...
DON'T! PLEASE. I SURRENDER.
I SURRENDER. JUST DON'T HURT ME ANYMORE.

YEAH. YOU WISH I WOULD SAY THAT, DON'T YOU? NEVER.
NO.
I WISH...
...I DIDN'T HAVE TO DO THIS.
NO!

AND AS FOR YOU...

...IT'S TIME TO END THIS.

THIS IS NOT RIGHT.

NOW WHAT?
THEY ARE TAKING CONTROL OF THE FEED AGAIN.
I AM NOT CERTAIN HOW.
LET THEM. ALL THEY CAN SHOW IS US WINNING, RIGHT?

"THIS IS YOUR HERO."
DON'T! PLEASE. I SURRENDER. I SURRENDER. JUST DON'T HURT ME ANYMORE.
NO!
THAT'S NOT HOW IT HAPPENED.
NINJA IS NOT YOUR HERO.

HE HAS BEEN LYING TO YOU. HE PRESENTS HIMSELF AS A HERO. AS YOU CAN SEE, HE IS ANYTHING BUT.
THIS IS SOME BULLCRAP.
HE'S LYING.
HE IS TRYING TO DISCREDIT YOU.
HE DOESN'T CARE ABOUT YOUR FREEDOM. HE DOESN'T CARE ABOUT YOUR SAFETY.
HE IS EVERYTHING THE KETTERUNG WAS DESIGNED TO SHOW US.
HE IS AN INSURGENT. WILLING TO DO ANYTHING...
...FOR MORE POWER.

HE'S LYING. THAT'S...THAT'S NOT WHAT HAPPENED. AT ALL.
HE CONTROLS THE FEED. SO HE CONTROLS TRUTH. OR AT LEAST WHAT SOME BELIEVE.

CAN'T YOU STOP THIS? CUT THE FEED?
I DO NOT KNOW. BUT EVEN IF POSSIBLE, I DO NOT KNOW IF IT IS WISE.

"NOT ALL HATE STRIGUS THULE."

YOU MUST UNDERSTAND. STRIGUS THULE CONQUERED, BUT WITH HIM HE BROUGHT A STABILITY. A CRUEL STABILITY, MADE FROM FEAR AND VIOLENCE BUT....

"...PEOPLE ARE AFRAID. CHAOS IS SOMETIMES WORSE THAN OPPRESSION.

"BUT MORE INSIDIOUS WAS WAY HE CONTROLLED INFORMATION. HE PRESENTED WORLD WHERE HE WAS SAVIOR. WHERE ONLY HE KNEW TRUTH."

AND SO MANY BELIEVED. MANY LOVED STRIGUS THULE. NOT ALL. NOT EVEN MOST. BUT ENOUGH.

THAT CAN'T BE RIGHT. PEOPLE WOULDN'T JUST BELIEVE LIES.
SOME PEOPLE ARE WEAK. CRUEL. LIKE KELLER. AND PEOPLE LIKE THAT,
THEY WILL TELL THEMSELVES ANYTHING TO BELIEVE THAT THEY ARE STRONG.

"EVEN IF THAT MEANS BELIEVING IN MONSTERS."

I CANNOT TAKE CONTROL OF FEED. THEY HAVE FOUND WAY TO LOCK ME OUT. I COULD CUT IT OFF, BUT IF I DO--
THEN IT JUST LOOKS LIKE I'M TRYING TO KEEP THEM FROM THE TRUTH.

IF I STOP THEM IT MAKES ME LOOK LIKE THE BAD GUY. IF I DON'T STOP THEM I LOOK LIKE THE BAD GUY.

BUT YOU AREN'T. AND THAT'S WHAT MATTERS. YOU--

YOU ARE HERO. EVERYONE WILL SEE.

THEY HAVE TO.

WE NEED THEM. WE CAN'T DO THIS ALONE. BUT KELLER... HIS STREAM WAS POPULAR. HE KNOWS HOW TO WORK THEM. SO HOW DO WE GET CONTROL BACK?

IF WE CAN GET TO SOURCE OF FEED, WE CAN TAKE CONTROL.
AWESOME, LET'S DO THAT.
I DO NOT KNOW HOW TO ENGAGE TRANSPORT.

YOU'RE A WHOLE LOT OF FUN, ZEPH.
I DO NOT KNOW WHERE IT IS. THAT DOESN'T MEAN I CANNOT FIND IT.
IF I HAVE MORE POWER, I MAY BE ABLE TO SEND A TRANSMISSION POWERFUL ENOUGH TO TRACE.
OKAY, GREAT, TERRIFIC. WE JUST NEED TO FIND MORE POWER.

GOOD NEWS, THEN.

I THINK IT'S BEING DELIVERED.

NINJA.
EVERYONE GET YOUR GAME FACES ON.
ON IT.

YOU DON'T NEED TO DO THIS. I KNOW YOU WERE LIKE US, ONCE. WHATEVER STRIGUS THULE HAS MADE YOU, YOU HAVE TO REMEMBER THAT.
HELP US.

IS THAT WHAT YOU TOLD CSDESIS BEFORE YOU STABBED HIM?

I DIDN'T WANT TO DO THAT.

BUT YOU DID. YOU DON'T EVEN DENY YOUR COWARDICE.
HE FOUGHT WITH HONOR.

YOU WILL DIE WITH NONE.
HOLY CRAP!
YOU ARE QUICK.
AHHH!
HE IS FAST.
YOU DON'T FREAKING SAY.
BUT NOT QUICK ENOUGH.

THEY WILL SEE YOU FOR WHAT YOU ARE. YOU WANT POWER. YOU WANT DOMINATION. YOU WANT TO SEE EVERYONE KNEEL TO YOU.
NO.
YOU SAY WE ARE THE SAME. WE ARE NOT. I SERVE MY MASTER. I BRING ORDER. PEACE. YOU BRING ONLY CHAOS.
NO!
SEE?
YOU ARE A THIEF, STEALING POWER THAT IS NOT YOURS.
I'M DONE TALKING.
YIELD. JOIN US.

NO.

WAIT, WHAT? IS HE--? IS HE ***RUNNING?***

INTERESTING.
I WOULD ADMIT THIS WAS UNEXPECTED.
I GUESS HE HEARD ABOUT US.

YOU NEED TO STOP.
IF YOU WANT TO STOP ME...

...CATCH ME. BECAUSE IF YOU DON'T, I WILL DESTROY EVERYTHING YOU CARE ABOUT.

I THOUGHT SO.

YOU THOUGHT WHAT? I COULDN'T FOLLOW?
WOULDN'T?

I THOUGHT YOU WOULD NOT FACE ME ALONE. WHERE IT IS SIMPLY POWER TO POWER. YOU ARE A COWARD, BUT PERHAPS NOT AS MUCH AS I WOULD HAVE THOUGHT. IT WILL BE FUN TO TAKE EVERYTHING FROM YOU.

DAMN YOU!
I'M NOT ALONE. AND IF YOU THINK THAT'S BAD...

...YOU'RE REALLY GOING TO HATE THIS.

NO!
SMASH
OKAY, THAT SUCKED.
OW.

ARE YOU UNHARMED?
DO YOU ALWAYS HAVE TO BITE MY LINES?
I WAS JUST--
NEVER MIND.
YOU OKAY, DUDE?

FOR A GIVEN VALUE OF OKAY, BETTER THAN THIS GUY.
WHAT IS YOUR NAME ANYWAY?

I AM KEDDIAS. I AM THE SCOURGE. I AM THE REAPER. I AM THE END.
AND YOU ARE A COWARD. THAT WAS THE KIND OF TRICK ONLY THE WEAK WOULD USE.

MAYBE. BUT I'M NOT THE ONE ON THE GROUND. NOW I THINK YOU KNOW THE NEXT LINE.
YIELD.

NEVER.

STOP. WE'RE DONE FIGHTING. GIVE UP OR GET GHOSTED.
NO OTHER OPTIONS.

HMMM.
KEDDIAS HAS TO GIVE UP.
HE WILL NOT. HE IS THE WORST OF THE GREAT BEASTS. HE DELIGHTS IN CRUELTY. HE CANNOT BE BARGAINED WITH.

I DON'T WANT TO DO THIS. DON'T MAKE ME DO THIS.

ARE YOU AFRAID TO LOOK ME IN THE EYE WHEN YOU DO IT?

LOOK AT HIM. HE'S NOT GOING TO STOP. HE LIKES IT.

THIS WAS THE PLAN. KELLER KNEW SOMETHING LIKE THIS WOULD HAPPEN. BUT WHAT OTHER CHOICE THERE.

DOZER IS RIGHT. THIS... CAN ONLY END ONE WAY.

BELIEVE ONE THING.
I WILL NEVER YIELD.
KEDDIAS.

I BELIEVE YOU.

AND DO YOU SEE?

AN OPPONENT RUN DOWN. AN HONORABLE MAN TRYING TO SURRENDER, ONLY TO BE STRUCK DOWN WHEN HE'S MOST VULNERABLE.
NINJA DOES NOT CARE ABOUT YOU. YOU ARE ONLY A TOOL TO GET WHAT HE MOST DESIRES:
MORE POWER.
I HAD TO.
KELLER WILL USE THIS AGAINST YOU, MAN.
YOU'LL LOOK LIKE A VILLAIN WHEN HE SPINS THIS. YOU WEREN'T SUPPOSED TO PLAY HIS GAME.
I DID WHAT I HAD TO DO.
THIS WAS THE ONLY WAY.

AND WAS THIS YOUR PLAN?
TO KEEP LOSING MY BROTHER'S GREATEST WEAPONS AND GIVE NINJA THEIR POWER?

"LOOK, ANNIS EPSILON.
"THEY ARE SEEING WHAT I WANT THEM TO SEE. NINJA AS A COWARD. A THIEF. A LIAR. NOT A SAVIOR.

"THEIR WILL IS BREAKING.

"AND THEY ARE RUNNING TO STRIGUS THULE TO SAVE THEM. TO GIVE THEM HOPE."

THAT IS MY PLAN. AND IT IS WORKING.
YOU KNEW HE WOULD LOSE. KEDDIAS.
YES.
AND YOU DON'T CARE.

LOSERS LOSE.
THEY'RE GOING TO ATTEMPT TO TRACK DOWN THE SOURCE OF THE FEED.
THAT'S ***HERE.***
YES.
WHERE WE ARE.
ANNIS.

YOU'RE LEADING THEM HERE.
YES.

I AM.

EVERYBODY BE ON GUARD. WE DON'T KNOW WHAT THEY'RE GOING TO THROW AT US NEXT. THIS COULD BE...
...DANGEROUS?
THIS IS DIFFERENT.
THIS IS NOT WHAT I WAS EXPECTING.
I'M NOT COMPLAINING. I DON'T LIKE FIGHTING. I MEAN, I **AM** AWESOME AT IT. BUT I DON'T LIKE IT.

THIS IS NOT THE REACTION HOPED FOR.
THEY DO NOT LOOK HAPPY.
I...SHOULD DO SOMETHING? SHOULD WE DO SOMETHING?
I BELIEVE THIS MAY BE THE ONLY OPPORTUNITY TO SHOW THEM SOMETHING OTHER THAN WHAT KELLER WANTS THEM TO SEE.
OKAY, RIGHT. YEAH...

...UH...
HELLO, I'M NINJA AND I'M HERE TO--

WHAT?

WE KNOW WHO YOU ARE.
WE KNOW WHAT YOU ARE.
IT'S NOT LIKE THAT. I DIDN'T... I AM TRYING TO HELP YOU. KELLER IS LYING TO YOU.
WE SAW YOU.
I GUESS THEY SAW THE FEED.
I'M TRYING TO HELP THEM.
I'M THINKING THEY DON'T WANT THE HELP.

WE SEE YOU UP THERE, THINKING YOU'RE ABOVE US. YOU THINK WE NEED YOU. YOU JUST WANT US TO KNEEL AND KISS YOUR FEET. YOU'RE NO DIFFERENT THAN THULE.

YOU *DO* NEED ME.
WAIT, NO, I DON'T MEAN IT LIKE THAT. I MEAN YOU--

I GUESS WE'LL SEE FOR OURSELVES.

THAT'S PROBABLY NOT A GOOD SIGN, RIGHT?
I'D LIKE TO THINK THEY HEARD ABOUT US AND DECIDED WE'RE TOO TOUGH TO TRY AND FIGHT, BUT I'M GUESSING WE'RE NOT THAT LUCKY.

NO...

...WE AREN'T.
TERRIFIC.
OKAY.
LET'S DO THIS.

THAT SPEAR IS A RANGED WEAPON. YOU NEED TO BE CAREFUL. I DON'T KNOW IF I CAN PROTECT YOU.
FEEL FREE TO PROTECT ME.
WHAT ARE THEY DOING?
NOTHING.
THEY ARE DOING...

"...NOTHING."

THEY ARE ERREDAN AND HESH.
THE FIERCEST OF THE GREAT BEASTS.
EVEN NEHERON FEARED THEM. BUT THIS IS... ODD.
ODD. RIGHT. OKAY, FINE, LET'S TRY THIS.

I'M ONLY GOING TO SAY THIS ONCE.
YIELD!

WE YIELD.
WAIT, WHAT?

WE YIELD.
WE SAW WHAT YOU HAVE DONE.
AND WHAT THIS NEW GREAT BEAST...
KELLER.
...CLAIMS YOU ARE DOING. BUT WE DO NOT BELIEVE HIM.

THIS IS A TRAP.
MAYBE.
OR SOME KIND OF OTHER ASSORTED TRICKERY.

HOW DO WE KNOW WE CAN TRUST YOU?

YOU DON'T.
AND WE DO NOT KNOW IF WE CAN TRUST YOU. PERHAPS YOU ARE WHAT THIS KELLER SAYS.
SO WE OFFER OURSELVES. WE ARE TIRED OF FIGHTING. YOU CAN STRIKE US DOWN, CLAIM OUR POWER AS YOUR OWN.
OR YOU CAN SPARE US. EITHER WAY, WE WILL KNOW WHO CAN BE TRUSTED.

THE CHOICE IS YOURS.

WE DO NOT YET HAVE THE POWER WE NEED.
I KNOW.
I CANNOT MAKE DECISION FOR YOU.
I KNOW THAT TOO. BUT IT'S OKAY. WHETHER I LIKE IT OR NOT...

...I KNOW WHAT I HAVE TO DO.

THE RIGHT THING.
AT LEAST I HOPE IT'S THE RIGHT THING. SO, I GUESS--
HI, I'M NINJA.

SMASH

OH, ISN'T THE FEED SHOWING YOU WHAT YOU WANT TO SEE?

IT WILL SHOW WHAT I TELL IT TO SHOW.

WE WERE ALWAYS A TEAM. AND WE WERE THE BEST.
AT ALL GAMES, BUT EVENTUALLY THE GAME.
AND SO WE WERE TAKEN TO THE KETTERUNG.
YOU KNOW THIS STORY, I THINK. THE ONLY THING DIFFERENT WAS THAT WE WERE THE LAST TWO PLAYERS.
"AND WE REFUSED TO FIGHT EACH OTHER.
"WE ASSUMED STRIGUS THULE WOULD KILL US, BUT IT DID NOT MATTER.
"HE DID NOT KILL US.
"BUT THE FIGHTING DIDN'T STOP BECAUSE WE WERE HIS NOW. THE GREAT BEASTS FIGHT AMONG EACH OTHER.
"AND WE BECAME WHAT WE HAD NEED TO BE. TO STAY TOGETHER."
TO SURVIVE.

OKAY.
WE CAN'T TRUST THEM. KELLER SENT THEM.

HE DID. BUT I BELIEVE THEM. WE'RE NOT BAD PEOPLE, RIGHT? AND WE MADE IT TO THE END OF THE GAME.
SO MAYBE NOT ALL THE GREAT BEASTS ARE BAD. MAYBE THEY ARE JUST GOOD PEOPLE PLACED IN A BAD WORLD.
YOU'RE RISKING A LOT ON MAYBE. WE NEED TO MAKE SURE WE WIN THIS.
OUR FRIENDS, OUR FAMILIES ARE BACK ON EARTH.
I KNOW. BUT IF YOU WANT TO WIN BIG, SOMETIMES YOU HAVE TO RISK BIG. IF THEY CAN HELP US, WE HAVE TO LET THEM.

I HAVE ENOUGH POWER. WE CAN PULSE TO THE FEED AND THE FEEDBACK WILL TELL US WHERE TRANSMISSION ORIGINATES.

AND THEN WHAT?

I'M SERIOUS. AND THEN WHAT?
WE TAKE OVER THE FEED.
AND THEN?
I...

WE NEED TO FIND THULE. OR GET HIM TO COME TO US. THAT'S "AND THEN WHAT."

THIS WILL BE DIFFICULT.
ZEPH, I AM NOT TOTALLY STUPID.
I KNOW THAT.
I BELIEVE YOU *THINK* YOU KNOW THAT.
BUT YOU NEED TO UNDERSTAND WHAT LIES AHEAD.

"IF WE MOVE QUICKLY ENOUGH HE WILL BE LIMITED IN HOW MANY SOLDIERS HE CAN BRING. BUT IT WILL STILL BE MANY.

"NIX AND B'LASNA WILL COME, TO STAND BETWEEN YOU AND THE TOWER. AND SHOULD YOU DEFEAT THEM...

"...KELLER AWAITS."

I GET IT. IT'S IMPOSSIBLE.
IS THAT WHAT YOU WANT ME TO SAY? I AM OPEN TO OTHER OPTIONS, BUT NO ONE HAS GIVEN ME ANY.
WHAT I AM SAYING IS YOU NEED TO BE PREPARED TO LOSE MUCH. YOU MUST SUCCEED, EVEN IF WE ALL FALL.
THAT'S NOT GOING TO HAPPEN.

I HAVE A QUESTION.
I GET WHY THULE WOULD PUT EVERYTHING HE CAN BETWEEN US AND THE FEED. BUT... HE ISN'T.
HE CALLS HIMSELF A GOD, RIGHT? WHY ISN'T HE STOPPING US? COULDN'T WE BE WALKING RIGHT INTO A FACE-TO-FACE WITH HIM?

WORSE. LIZA FOUND A WAY TO MAKE IT WORSE. SOMEHOW.
I DO NOT BELIEVE THAT HE WILL.
I HAVE WATCHED THULE FOR MANY YEARS. I BELIEVE I KNOW HIS WAYS.

IT WOULD NOT BE ENOUGH TO DEFEAT YOU. HE CRAVES...CHALLENGE. HE WANTS YOU TO SUCCEED ONLY SO YOU HAVE FURTHER TO FALL.
HE WANTS YOU STRONG. SO YOUR DEFEAT HURTS.

WELL, THAT'S NOT HAPPENING. BLOW THE FEED.

THOOM

AH!

FIRST HE SMASHES IT AND NOW THEY BLOW IT UP.
WHAT HAPPENED?
THEY SENT A SURGE OF AKASHIC ENERGY. IT BLEW EVERY-THING. THEY--

THEY'RE COMING.

NO NO NO. THEY BLEW THE NONSPACE SHIFTER.
WHY DID YOU LEAVE ME HERE, BROTHER? WAS THIS THE PLAN? I AM JUST A TOY? IS THIS ANOTHER GAME?
WE CAN REPAIR, BUT WE WILL NEED TIME.
REPAIR THE SHIFTER FIRST.
"THAT FOOL KELLER CAN DEAL WITH THIS."

I AM GIVING YOU ONE CHANCE TO SURRENDER.
I GUESS THAT QUALIFIES AS AN ANSWER.

WE'LL TRY TO LEAVE SOME FOR YOU.
I ADMIT, THIS IS AT LEAST EXCITING, YES?
I--
LOOK OUT!
GREAT.
YOU ARE WELCOME. I HOPE THEY DO LEAVE SOME FOR US.
YEAH, WELL--

DON'T THINK THAT'S GOING TO BE A PROBLEM.
KEEP THEM FOCUSED ON US.
I DON'T THINK THAT WILL BE AN ISSUE.
YEAH, A LITTLE HELP HERE.

OKAY, THIS MIGHT BE TOO FOCUSED ON US.
EXCITING. I AM LIKING THESE NEW WEAPONS.
YOU AND I ARE VERY DIFFERENT PEOPLE.
YOU KNOW YOU CAN STOP. JUST...QUIT. WALK AWAY. BECAUSE IF YOU KEEP FIGHTING, THIS ISN'T GOING TO GO WELL FOR YOU. I--

AH!

HEH.
WELCOME!

I HAVE YOU.
AND I HAVE THIS.

THAT ISN'T GOOD.
THAT IS NOT OUR BATTLE. ***THIS*** IS OUR BATTLE.

YOU ARE LUCKY.
I REALLY DON'T FEEL LUCKY.
NIX RARELY HAS TO STRIKE TWICE.

I HOPE YOU ARE ABLE TO FIGHT...

BECAUSE A FIGHT HAS ARRIVED.

SOMETHING IS WRONG. WHERE ARE THE OTHERS? THEY SHOULD BE HERE.
WELL, GOOD NEWS...
...THEY ARE.
EVERYONE RUN! EVERYONE BUT EPSILON.
SO THIS WAS A DISTRACTION? KEEP THE FORCES FOCUSED OUTSIDE WHILE YOU TAKE OVER THE FEED FROM THE INSIDE?
CLEVER.
I AM GOOD AT CLEVER.
LET US SEE WHAT ELSE YOU ARE GOOD AT.

YOU ARE FAST! THAT IS GOOD!

CAN YOU FIGHT, HESH?
FOR YOU? ALWAYS.
YOU HAVE NOT TOLD ME TO YIELD?
IS THE GREAT BEAST B'LASNA UNWORTHY?
W...WOULD YOU?
HAHA! NO! BUT IT'S NICE TO BE ASKED.
HAD TO TRY.

I SUPPOSE YOU THOUGHT THAT I WAS SIMPLY STRIGUS THULE'S VOICE.
THE MOUTH OF THE ZERO BEAST.
SHE'S STRONG.
I AM ANNIS EPSILON.
AND WHILE I AM NOT MY BROTHER...
...I AM MORE THAN CAPABLE OF DEFENDING MYSELF AGAINST YOU.
SO NOW TELL ME...
...DO YOU HAVE ANY OTHER CLEVER IDEAS?

HAHA! WELL DONE! I KNEW THE GREAT HESH WOULD NOT FALL EASILY.
SEE IF YOU CAN DO SOMETHING ABOUT THESE FREAKING ARROWS, HB.
I DIDN'T KNOW THAT HEADBANDS COULD DO THAT.
...
STOP.

I AM IMPRESSED. YOU MANAGED TO HIDE FOR YEARS, ZEPHYR.
IT WOULD HAVE BEEN INTERESTING TO HEAR HOW.

YOU ARE LESS IMPRESSIVE.
WILLING TO BETRAY YOUR FRIENDS FOR A CHANCE TO WIN.
IS THIS MEANT TO BE REDEMPTION?

BECAUSE YOU ARE DOING A VERY POOR JOB OF IT.

JUST... BUYING... TIME.

WHAT--
YOU ASKED ME TO DO SOMETHING CLEVER.

HERE IT IS.

YOU SHOULD BE HAPPY! THIS IS GLORIOUS!
DO YOU EVER STOP TALKING?
HE DOES NOT.
RELEASE ME, YOU WRETCHED PIECE OF HEADWEAR.
BRRAHH!
ENOUGH.
YEAH...
...YOU'RE RIGHT ABOUT THAT.

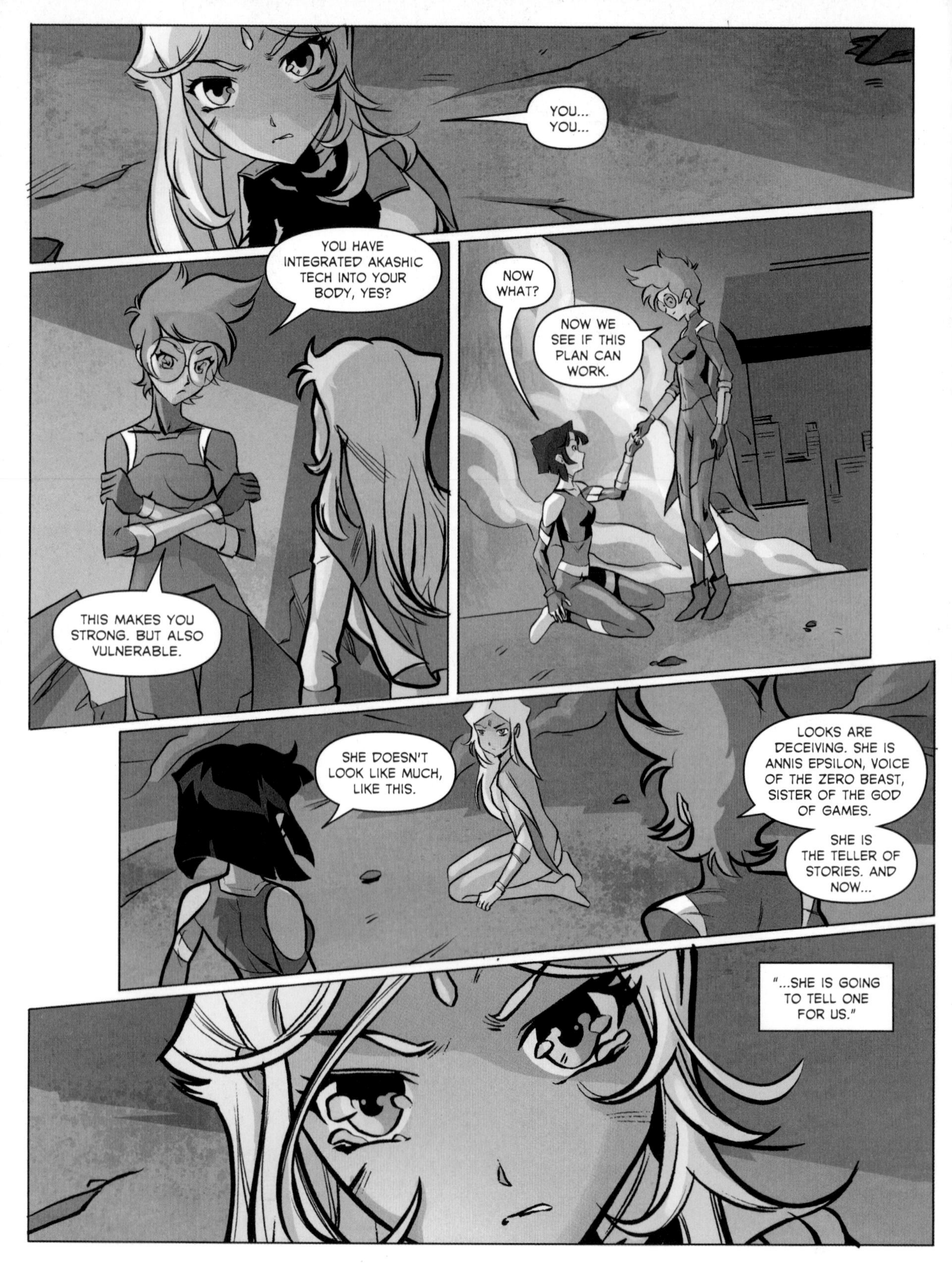
YOU... YOU...
YOU HAVE INTEGRATED AKASHIC TECH INTO YOUR BODY, YES?
THIS MAKES YOU STRONG. BUT ALSO VULNERABLE.
NOW WHAT?
NOW WE SEE IF THIS PLAN CAN WORK.
SHE DOESN'T LOOK LIKE MUCH, LIKE THIS.
LOOKS ARE DECEIVING. SHE IS ANNIS EPSILON, VOICE OF THE ZERO BEAST, SISTER OF THE GOD OF GAMES.
SHE IS THE TELLER OF STORIES. AND NOW...
"...SHE IS GOING TO TELL ONE FOR US."

YOU.
YOU CANNOT POSSIBLY BELIEVE THAT THIS IS A FIGHT YOU CAN WIN. I AM GREAT BEAST TWO AND YOU...
JUST PLAYERS.
YOU ARE NOTHING. THIS IS BENEATH ME.
BUT SOMETIMES NECESSITY CALLS.

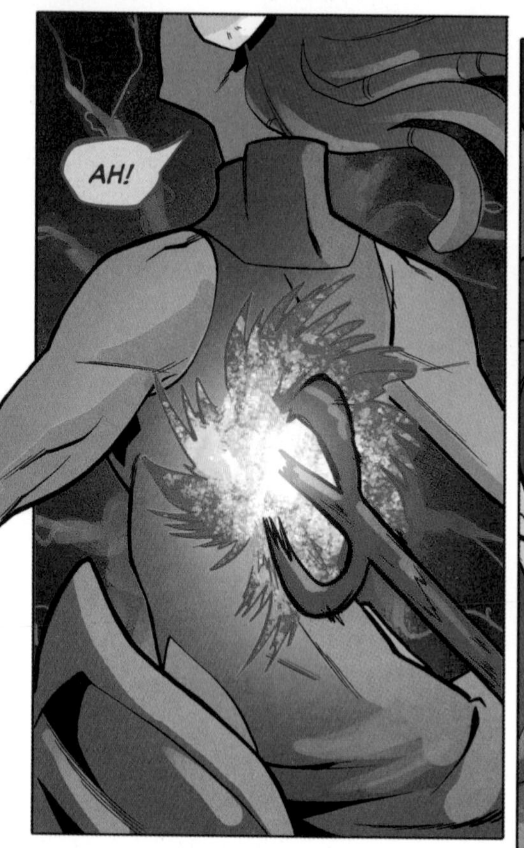
AH!

HELLO, NIX.

RAAAHHHH!
THIS IS NOT BETTER.

IN THE BACK? I NEVER TOOK YOU FOR A COWARD, ERREDAN.
CONSIDER IT A COMPLIMENT. FOR YOU, I WILL TAKE ANY ADVANTAGE I CAN FIND.

HE'S CHARGING AS FAST AS I CAN DRAIN HIM. YOU CAN'T...

NO.
YES!

HESH!

YOU WERE ALWAYS EACH OTHER'S STRENGTH...

"...AND YOUR WEAKNESS."
I WAS HOPING FOR BETTER.
BUT THIS WILL HAVE TO DO.
NO, I DO NOT THINK IT WILL.
YOU.
NO.

US.
STOP MOVING.
ALL OF US.
UH. NO?
YOU REALLY SHOULD TURN AROUND.
EVEN I AM NOT THAT STUPID.
YOU KNOW...

I REALLY THINK YOU ARE.
NO!
KELLER. YOU'VE CHANGED. BUT YOU HAVEN'T CHANGED AT ALL.

DIE!

NO.

I DON'T BELIEVE I WILL.

I WAS WONDERING WHERE YOU WERE.

DO YOU KNOW WHAT YOU DID WHEN YOU BLEW THE FEED?
RUINED YOUR PLAN TO MAKE ME LOOK LIKE THE BAD GUY?

NO.
YOU MADE IT SO STRIGUS THULE COULDN'T HEAR OR SEE US.

WHICH MEANS I CAN TELL YOU THIS. THIS WAS NEVER ABOUT *YOU.*
IT'S ALWAYS BEEN ABOUT ME. YOU'VE ALWAYS BEEN DOGGING ME. TRYING TO BE ME.

HAH. WELL, YOU'RE NOT WRONG.
BUT THIS? ALL THIS, THE KETTERUNG, STRIGUS THULE, THE THOUSAND DOMINIONS. IT'S OPENED MY EYES.
IF I SERVE AS GREAT BEAST SEVEN, THEN I WILL ALWAYS BE IN HIS SHADOW. I WILL ALWAYS BE SECOND.

BUT, YOU. YOU GAVE ME OPPORTUNITY. THERE'S CHAOS IN THE DOMINIONS. THULE'S FORCES ARE SCATTERED.
HIS FEED IS DOWN. AND NOW, THANKS TO YOU, THERE IS ONLY ONE GREAT BEAST LEFT.

AFTER I GHOST YOU, AND I ***WILL*** GHOST YOU, THERE WILL BE NOTHING IN THE WAY OF ME TAKING STRIGUS THULE'S THRONE. AND HE WON'T EVER SEE IT COMING.

TWO THINGS.
ONE: YOU ALWAYS DID TALK TOO MUCH.
AND TWO:

HE IS *DEFINITELY* GOING TO SEE IT COMING.

WE'RE BACK!
GOOD. RUN THE FOOTAGE. I WILL NOT HAVE MUCH TIME FOR NEXT PART. I HAVE REMOVED THE SHIFTER CONTROL FROM ANNIS EPSILON, BUT I WILL NEED TIME.

NO.

OH, YES. YOU ADMITTING HOW YOU LIED ABOUT ME? YOUR PLAN TO BETRAY STRIGUS THULE? WE GOT IT. ALL OF IT.

HE WILL NEVER SEE IT COMING.

YOU THINK THAT MATTERS? I CAN STILL GHOST YOU.

MAYBE. HECK, PROBABLY.

BUT I THINK...

"...YOU'RE ALL OUT OF TIME."

GET READY, GRAB ANY WEAPON YOU CAN. THIS IS GOING TO GET UGLY.
ARE YOU... ARE YOU ABOUT READY?
NO. WE WILL NEED TIME.
I DON'T THINK YOU'RE GOING TO GET IT. I NEED TO GO OUT THERE AND PROTECT NINJA.
STRIGUS THULE.
YOU CAN PROTECT HIM MORE BY DOING THE TASK SET TO YOU. WHEN IT IS TIME, PLAY WHAT WE HAVE PREPARED.
I KNOW. BUT IT'S GOING TO WORK. IT HAS TO.
STRIGUS THULE. THE GOD OF GAMES. THE ZERO BEAST.

DIE!

HOLLAND KELLER.

THIS IS THE LESSON.

PEOPLE WILL ALWAYS FIGHT. ALWAYS BETRAY. ALWAYS WAR.
THIS IS THE LESSON OF THE GAME. THIS IS THE GIFT I HAVE GIVEN THE THOUSAND DOMINIONS.

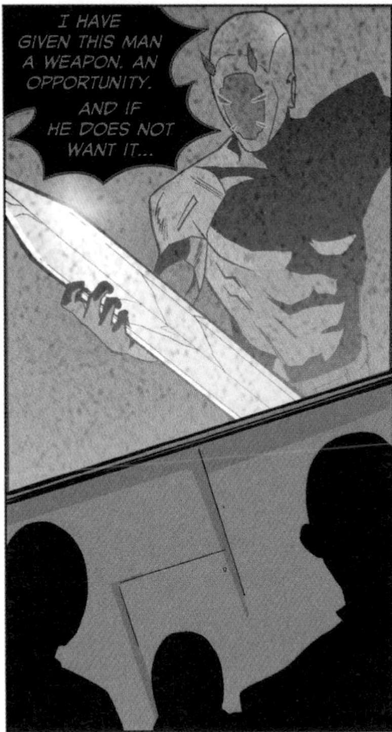
I HAVE GIVEN THIS MAN A WEAPON. AN OPPORTUNITY.
AND IF HE DOES NOT WANT IT...

...I CAN TAKE IT AWAY.

AND IF HE DOES NOT WANT THE POWER I GAVE HIM...

...I CAN TAKE THAT AWAY TOO.

NO.

NINJA, I--
YOU CAN'T DO THIS. WE'RE NOT TOYS.
AND WHO WOULD STOP ME?
YOU?

NO.
NO, I DIDN'T THINK SO.

NO ONE IS COMING TO SAVE YOU.

YOU ARE ALREADY SAVED. I AM STRIGUS THULE. I AM THE ZERO BEAST.

AND NO ONE CAN STAND AGAINST ME.

STRIGUS THULE.

HE CALLS HIMSELF THE GOD OF GAMES. THE ZERO BEAST. THE GREAT UNITER. HE CALLS HIMSELF MANY THINGS...

"...BUT I CALL HIM BROTHER.
"THE KETTERUNG WAS OUR HOME. IT WAS DIFFERENT THEN, ALL THOSE CENTURIES PAST. A WARMER PLACE. AND A HAPPIER ONE.
"NO MATTER WHAT I TRIED.
"HE ALWAYS FELT... LESSER, I SUPPOSE. WEAK.
"INSECURE. AND HE RETREATED INTO HIS GAMES.
"OUR FATHER WAS BRILLIANT MAN. BEYOND BRILLIANT. AND DRIVEN.

"FOR SOME AT LEAST.
"BUT STRIGUS. HE WAS NEVER HAPPY. THERE WAS ALWAYS A HOLE IN HIM THAT COULD NEVER BE FILLED.
"NO MATTER WHAT OUR PARENTS TRIED.
"I SUPPOSE THAT WAS WHY HE WAS THE ONE WHO DISCOVERED AKASHIC ENERGY. PURE POWER FROM THE NONSPACE BETWEEN DOMINIONS, ALTHOUGH WE DIDN'T YET UNDERSTAND THAT.
"AND MY BROTHER, FOR ALL HIS FAULTS, HAD A GIFT FOR THIS THAT I DID NOT. WE THOUGHT... I THOUGHT... THAT PERHAPS THIS WOULD HAVE GIVEN HIM THE PURPOSE HE NEVER HAD.
"I WAS MORE RIGHT THAN I COULD HAVE IMAGINED.
"MY FATHER SAW IN AKASHIC TECHNOLOGY CLEAN POWER. AN END TO SCARCITY. ENDLESS HOPE. MY BROTHER...
"...HE SAW SOMETHING ELSE."

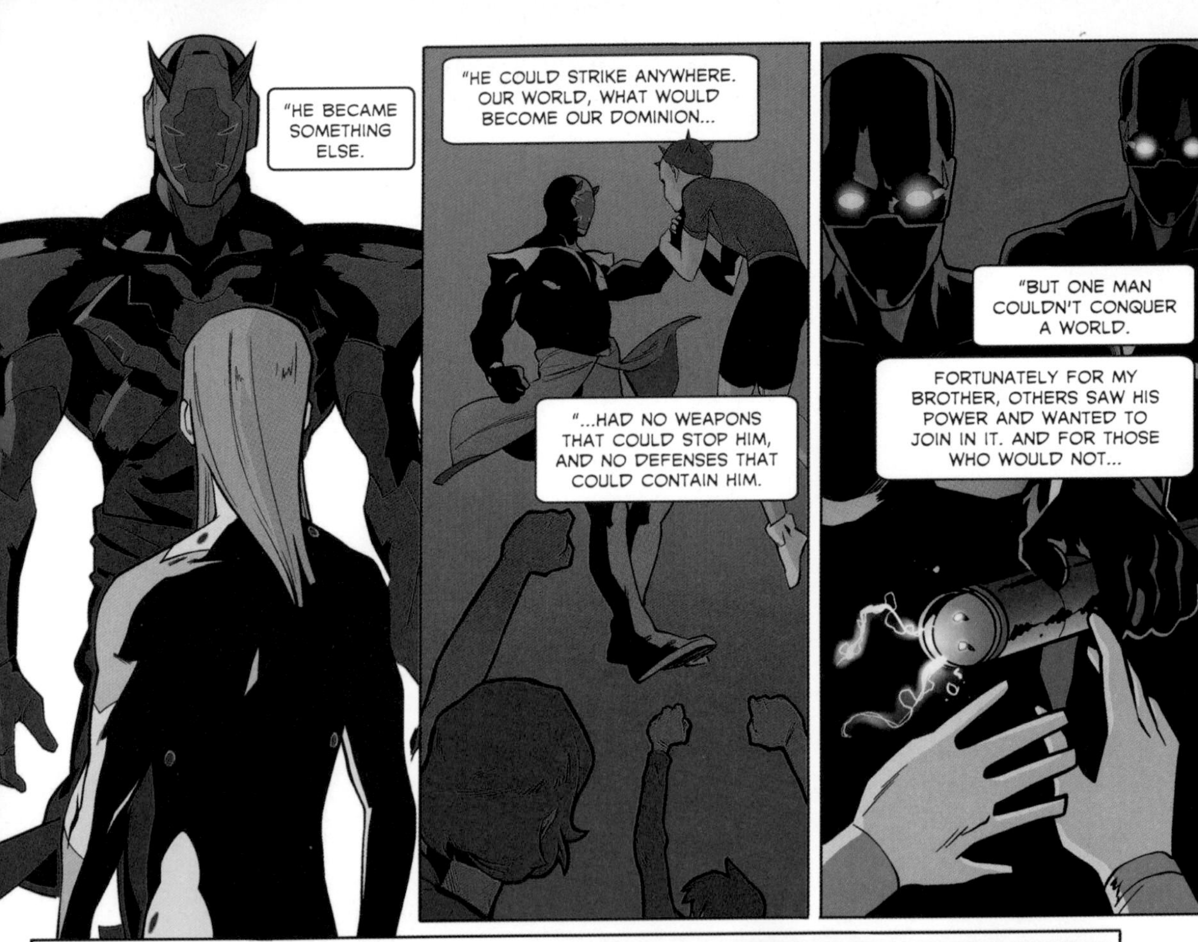
"HE BECAME SOMETHING ELSE.
"HE COULD STRIKE ANYWHERE. OUR WORLD, WHAT WOULD BECOME OUR DOMINION...
"...HAD NO WEAPONS THAT COULD STOP HIM, AND NO DEFENSES THAT COULD CONTAIN HIM.
"BUT ONE MAN COULDN'T CONQUER A WORLD.
FORTUNATELY FOR MY BROTHER, OTHERS SAW HIS POWER AND WANTED TO JOIN IN IT. AND FOR THOSE WHO WOULD NOT...

"...THEY COULD BE PERSUADED."

OUR WORLD FELL.
BUT AS MY BROTHER SOON DISCOVERED, OURS WAS NOT THE ONLY WORLD...

"...AND MY BROTHER STILL HUNGERED.
"HE ALWAYS LOVED GAMES. HE CONVERTED THE KETTERUNG, RAVAGED AND ABANDONED, INTO A PLACE WHERE HE COULD BREAK THOSE WHO COULD OPPOSE HIM.
"HE CREATED THE GREAT BEASTS AS SYMBOLS OF HIS MIGHT. THE STRONGEST HE COULD FIND, CONVERTED INTO TOOLS.
"AND HE CREATED THE FEED TO MAKE SURE THAT NO ONE COULD FORGET OR DOUBT."
BUT I NEVER FORGOT WHAT HE WAS. BENEATH THE POWER. BENEATH THE ARMOR AND THE ARMIES.

MY LITTLE BROTHER.
DOOM!

I REALLY, REALLY HOPE YOU'RE ABOUT READY, BECAUSE ANOTHER ONE LIKE THAT AND THIS BUILDING IS COMING DOWN ON OUR HEADS.
I AM ALMOST THERE.
GET READY. THEY WANTED TO RATTLE HIM. IT LOOKS LIKE IT WORKED.
AND THAT IS GOOD A THING?
WELL...
"...I GUESS WE'RE GOING TO FIND OUT."
THEY SEE YOU, THULE.
EVERYONE, IN ALL THE DOMINIONS.
THEY SEE HOW WEAK YOU REALLY ARE. HOW YOU ONLY HAVE POWER OVER THEM AS LONG AS THEY *THINK* YOU DO.
YOU--

NO.

NOW!

I NEED TO--
GO.
ARE YOU SURE? I'M SUPPOSED TO PROTECT YOU.
I NO LONGER NEED PROTECTION. BUT OTHERS WILL. GO.

I WILL NOT SIMPLY KILL YOU.

I GOT THIS.
DOZER, DON'T!

I WILL TEAR YOU OUT OF HISTORY. NO RECORD WILL REMAIN. NO MEMORY.

YOU WILL BE NOTHING. YOU WILL BE NO ONE.

IT DOESN'T MATTER.

YES...

...YOU ARE RIGHT ABOUT THAT. YOU DON'T MATTER.
YOU ACTUALLY SUCCEEDED IN MAKING ME ANGRY. IT'S BEEN CENTURIES SINCE ANYONE HAS MORE THAN ANNOYED ME.
YOU ARE GOING TO REGRET THAT.

YES.

YOU THOUGHT THIS COULD DEFEAT ME? AND WHAT?
SHOW THE DOMINIONS THAT I AM VULNERABLE?
IT WAS A CLEVER PLAN. BUT LOOK WHAT CLEVER GOT YOU.
I KNEW WE COULDN'T BEAT YOU.
WE JUST NEEDED TO DISTRACT YOU SO THAT YOU WOULDN'T NOTICE THE AKASHIC ENERGY DRAIN.

WHAT DID YOU DO?
I SAID NO, WHEN YOU ASKED ME IF I THOUGHT I COULD DEFEAT YOU.
YOU SAID NO ONE COULD DEFEAT YOU. YOU WERE RIGHT...

...NO ONE COULD.

IT WON'T MATTER. AND YOU WON'T BE THERE TO SEE IT.
YEAH, WELL...

...SPEAKING OF NOT SEEING THINGS...
WHUMP

...YOU'VE GOT A HABIT OF FOCUSING ON THE WRONG THINGS.
YOU.

NAH...

US.

ARE YOU ABLE TO FIGHT?
I AM PRETTY SURE HE SLAPPED MY DAMN SOUL OUT OF ME, BUT IF MY FRIENDS ARE FIGHTING, THEN I'M FIGHTING.

NOW WHAT?
NOW...

"...A REALLY BIG FIGHT."

YOU DO NOT MATTER.

THIS DOES NOT MATTER.

YOU WILL NOT WIN. YOU--

ENOUGH.
WHAM

WE NEED TO GET IN THERE.
WE NEED TO WAIT.
FOR WHAT?
FOR THE RIGHT MOMENT.

YOU THINK THE WEAPONS I GAVE YOU CAN BE USED AGAINST ME?

I AM THE GOD OF GAMES.

AND I DO NOT LOSE.

I WILL NOT ALLOW THIS TO CONTINUE.

YOU ARE DONE. THIS IS DONE.
NOW WHERE IS NINJA? HE--

WHAM
HE'S RIGHT HERE.
NOBODY GETS TO LAUNCH ME AND WALK AWAY.
YOU CAN BEAT ANY OF US.
BUT NOT ALL OF US.

IS THAT SO?

CRAP!

ANY OF YOU. ALL OF YOU.

IT WILL ALWAYS END THE SAME WAY.

NO!
KEEP ON HIM. WE CAN DO THIS.
YOU WILL DO NOTHING.

BUT FAIL.
CRUNCH

THIS ISN'T...CAN'T END THIS WAY.

STOP!

I INTEND TO STOP THIS--

AS DO I.

NO.

YES. ALL THAT POWER? *YOUR* POWER?

"THAT'S OUR POWER NOW."
WHOA.

THIS IS MORE LIKE IT, I THINK.

IT FEELS... AWESOME.

WHAT... WHAT DID YOU DO?

ZEPH KNEW YOU WERE ABLE TO CHANNEL AKASHIC ENERGY DIRECTLY. IF WE'RE LIKE BATTERIES, THEN YOU'RE LIKE A GENERATOR.
NOW THOUGH? THE MORE POWER YOU DRAW...

...THE STRONGER WE GET.
IT WILL NOT BE... ENOUGH.
EVERYONE...
NOW
DOZER, A LITTLE HELP?
GET READY.
GOT IT.

BECAUSE I'M GOING TO DROP THE HAMMER.

NO!

I ALWAYS WIN. I AM--

A LOSER. YOU WERE ALWAYS A LOSER.
AND NOW EVERYONE IS GOING TO KNOW.

DIE.

NO.

NO ONE
DIES.

NOT EVEN
YOU.

CRUNCH

NO. NONONONO NONO.
YOU'RE GOING TO LIVE **WITH** THIS.
WITH ALL THE WORLD SEEING YOU AS YOU REALLY ARE, STRIPPED OF ARMOR AND ARMIES.
YOU HAD TO LIE ABOUT ME TO BREAK PEOPLE'S FAITH IN ME. AND I ALMOST BROKE MYSELF. BUT FOR YOU? ALL I HAVE TO DO IS SHOW THEM THE TRUTH.
THIS IS STRIGUS THULE.
THIS IS WHAT HE REALLY IS. ALL HE EVER WAS. A BOY WHO NEVER GREW UP. WHO HID BEHIND TECHNOLOGY AND CONVINCED YOU TO BE AFRAID OF HIM.
REAL POWER LIES IN YOU. IN ALL OF US, WORKING TOGETHER.
NOT LETTING PEOPLE LIKE HIM DIVIDE US. AND IF THE DOMINIONS CAN WORK TOGETHER, WE CAN ALL BE FREE.

"THULE IS UNDER CONSTANT FEED SURVEILLANCE. THE DOMINIONS NEED THAT. BUT HE HASN'T SPOKEN, HASN'T MOVED. I DO NOT THINK HE KNOWS HOW TO LIVE IN THE REAL WORLD.
"ANNIS EPSILON HAS BEEN PROTESTING THAT SHE WAS COERCED. UNLIKE HER BROTHER, SHE DOES NOTHING BUT SPEAK. IT IS NOT CONVINCING.
"KELLER...IS A PROBLEM. IT WAS TOO CRUEL TO LEAVE HIM GHOSTED.
"BUT WE CANNOT SEND HIM BACK TO YOUR DOMINION, I DO NOT THINK.
"THE REST OF THE GREAT BEASTS HAVE BEEN RETURNED TO THEIR NATURAL STATES, BUT THEY TOO REMAIN IN HOLDING.
"I BELIEVE THEY WOULD NOT BE SAFE IF RETURNED HOME.
"HESH AND ERREDAN RENOUNCED THEIR POWER WILLINGLY, AND SUBMITTED TO BEING HELD. THERE WILL BE TRIALS FOR ALL OF THEM. AND PUNISHMENT. BUT I THINK IT WILL BE LIGHT FOR THOSE TWO."

SO THOSE PROBLEMS ARE UNDER CONTROL.
THERE ARE MANY, MANY, MANY OTHER PROBLEMS LINED UP BEHIND THEM. THE THOUSAND DOMINIONS NEED A GOVERNMENT.
WE MUST DECIDE WHAT IS TO BE DONE WITH THULE'S SOLDIERS, HIS COLLABORATORS. WE MUST...
...WE MUST BUILD A FUTURE.
YEP.
THE DOMINIONS NEED A LEADER.
YEP.
I WAS MEANING YOU.
OH, I GOT THAT. HERE'S THE THING ABOUT THAT...
...THEY'VE ALREADY GOT ONE.
WHAT?
I'M A STREAMER. GAMER. THAT'S WHO I REALLY AM. A NORMAL GUY FROM A NORMAL PLACE.
BUT TO THE DOMINIONS, I'M NINJA, THE MAN WHO BEAT STRIGUS THULE. A LEGEND. IF I STAYED HERE, I WOULDN'T BE A LEADER. I'D BE A RULER. AND AS GOOD OF ONE AS I'D TRY TO BE, THAT'S NOT WHAT THEY NEED.
YOU ARE WHAT THEY NEED. YOU WERE THE ONE WHO MADE THIS POSSIBLE. YOU'RE THE ONE WHO CAN LEAD THEM. IT'S YOU, ZEPHYR. IT'S ALWAYS BEEN YOU.
I AM NOT READY.
NO ONE COULD BE. NOW...

"... CAN YOU PLEASE SEND US HOME?"
YOU ALL READY?
I WAS READY TWO DAYS AGO WHEN WE SENT EVERYONE ELSE HOME.
YOU'RE THE ONE WHO'S BEEN LOITERING.
AND I NEED, LIKE, ALL THE SHOWERS AND THEN TWO, MAYBE THREE WEEKS OF SLEEP.

I AM SENDING YOU BACK TO YOUR LAST KNOWN LOCATIONS ON EARTH. I CAN DO NOTHING ABOUT THE TIME THAT HAS PASSED. I AM SORRY.
WE WILL MISS YOU.

WELL, IF YOU NEED ME...

...YOU KNOW WHERE TO FIND ME.

SO, HB, WELCOME TO EARTH.
NO, IT DOESN'T ALL LOOK LIKE THIS. MAN, EVERYONE IS CRITIC.

BZZZZ
DOZER: Home.
My cat is mad. But my roommate fed him. No idea what I'm going to tell him. Or anyone.
The truth?
Oh, you're funny.

LIZARD: That all really happened, right?
Yep.
Can we pretend it didn't?
Honestly, I'd just settle for it not happening again.

TYLER "NINJA" BLEVINS is a professional gamer, streamer, and content creator. He is massively popular for playing *Fortnite* (which boasts forty million players per month), though he initially gained his fanbase by competing in professional *Halo* tournaments. After quitting esports to become a streamer, he played various First-Person Shooter Battle Royale games (such as *H1Z1* and *PUBG*), but found his big break with *Fortnite*. His energetic, entertaining persona and unmatched gaming prestige have garnered him tens of millions of followers worldwide.

JUSTIN JORDAN has penned comics for Image, DC, and Marvel Comics, as well as the *Call of Duty: Zombies* graphic novels for Dark Horse Books and *Urban Animal* on Webtoon. In 2012, he was nominated for the Harvey Award for Most Promising New Talent and is one of the writers of the Eisner-nominated *In the Dark: A Horror Anthology* and *Where We Live: A Benefit for the Survivors in Las Vegas*.

MIKE ANDERSON is a comic book artist and animator from Oklahoma, where he lives with his wife and kids.

FELIPE MAGAÑA is a character designer and concept artist for comics and video games.

Published in the United States by Ten Speed Press, an imprint of Random House, a division of Penguin Random House LLC, New York.
www.tenspeed.com

Ten Speed Press and the Ten Speed Press colophon are registered trademarks of Penguin Random House LLC.

Library of Congress Control Number: 2020951250

Trade Paperback ISBN: 978-1-9848-5746-0
eBook ISBN: 978-1-9848-5747-7

Printed in China

Acquiring editor: Aaron Wehner | Project editor: Kimmy Tejasindhu
Art direction and designer: Chloe Rawlins
Colorist: Brad Simpson
Letterer: Carlos Mangual
Production manager: Jane Chinn
Copyeditor(s): Mark Burstein | Proofreader(s): Carol Burrell
Publicist: Lauren Kretzschmar | Marketer: Daniel Wikey

10 9 8 7 6 5 4 3 2 1

First Edition